The
OCEAN
Alphabet Book

Jerry Pallotta • Illustrated by Frank Mazzola, Jr.

 Charlesbridge

Published by Charlesbridge
85 Main Street, Watertown, MA 02472
(617) 926-0329 • www.charlesbridge.com

Library of Congress Cataloging-in-Publication Data
Pallotta, Jerry.
  The ocean alphabet book / by Jerry Pallotta; Frank Mazzola, Jr.
illustrator.
        p.   cm.
  Summary: Introduces the letters A to Z by describing fish and other creatures living in
the North Atlantic Ocean.
  ISBN-13: 978-0-88106-458-2; ISBN-10: 0-88106-458-0 (reinforced for library use)
  ISBN-13: 978-0-88106-452-0; ISBN-10: 0-88106-452-1 (softcover)
1. Marine fauna—Juvenile literature. 2. English language—Alphabet—Juvenile literature.
[1. Marine animals. 2. Alphabet.] I. Mazzola, Frank, ill. II. Title.
QL122.2.P35   1991
591.92—dc20   89-60424

Printed in Korea
(hc) 10 9 8 7 6 5 4 3 2 1
(sc) 10 9 8 7 6 5 4

This book is dedicated to Nicolas and Jeffery Pallotta.

A a

A is for Alphabet book.
A is also for Atlantic Ocean. The fish and other creatures in this book live in the North Atlantic Ocean.

Bb

B is for Bluefish. Everyone loves to catch Bluefish because they love to fight. Their teeth are very, very sharp, so don't ever put your fingers in their mouths.

Cc

C is for Cod. Cod can be found everywhere in the North Atlantic Ocean. Some grow to be as big as a ten-year-old boy or girl.

Dd

D is for Dogfish. They are also known as Spiny Dogfish. They are little sharks. Every Dogfish has a barb on its back and a barb on its tail.

Ee

E is for Eel. Eels are slimy! Eels are long and thin like snakes. If you do not like to hold snakes, then you probably would not like to hold Eels.

Ff

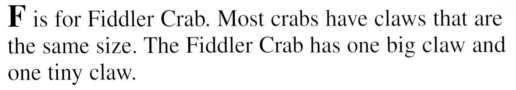

F is for Fiddler Crab. Most crabs have claws that are the same size. The Fiddler Crab has one big claw and one tiny claw.

G is for Goosefish. A Goosefish is ugly-looking. It has lots of teeth. Its mouth is as wide as its body. Goosefish are also called monkfish.

Gg

Hh

H is for Haddock. A Haddock looks a lot like a Cod. Behind the Haddock's side fin there is a dark spot that looks like a fingerprint.

I is for Inkfish. Inkfish is another name for squid. Squid spray ink to scare away fish that attack them.

Ii

J j

J is for Jellyfish. Jellyfish are soft, gooey, and see-through. Their dangling arms can sting if you touch them.

K is for Killer Whale. Killer Whales are mammals. They are not fish. They are very beautiful and can jump completely out of the water.

Kk

L l

L is for Lobster. Lobsters are reddish-green and blue. When they are cooked th[ey] turn bright red. They have two claws tha[t] can pinch. They have eight legs. They al[so] have two antennas that help them find o[ut] where they are.

Mm

M is for Minnow. Minnows are little fish. Usually they are only as big as your fingers. They can be found in shallow waters, marshlands, and creeks.

Nn

N is for Northern Puffer. If you touch a Puffer, it will blow itself up like a balloon.

Oo

O is for Octopus. This Octopus is scary-looking, but it will not hurt you. It has eight arms. Can you imagine shaking hands with an Octopus? It would take all day!

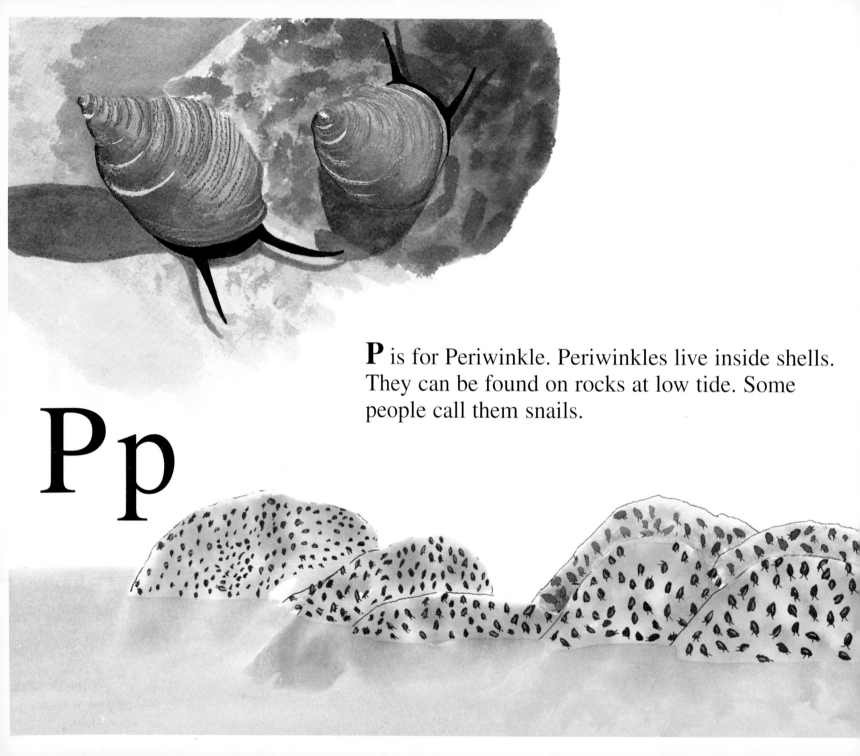

Pp

P is for Periwinkle. Periwinkles live inside shells. They can be found on rocks at low tide. Some people call them snails.

Q q

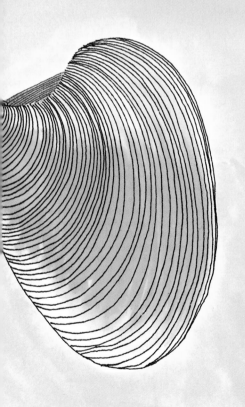

Q is for Quahog. Quahogs are clams that have hard shells.
Seagulls manage to open them all by themselves. Small
Quahogs are called cherrystones and littlenecks.

Rr

R is for Redfish. Redfish are caught in very deep water. They are oily, and lobstermen use them as bait to catch lobsters.

S s

S is for Scallop. Scallops are like clams, and they have pretty shells. There are many other creatures whose names begin with S: Sharks, Sculpins, Salmon, Sand Dollars, Sunfish, Smelt, Sea Snails, Skates, Shrimp, and Starfish.

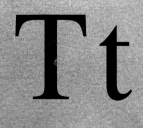

Tt

T is for Tuna. Everbody has heard of Tuna. When they are grown-up, they are almost as big as cars.

Uu

U is for Urchin. Urchins are round with hundreds of sharp little spines sticking out of their shells. If you are barefoot, try not to step on one!

V v

V is for Viperfish. Viperfish live in deep, dark waters. They have lights inside their mouths and along their sides to attract food.

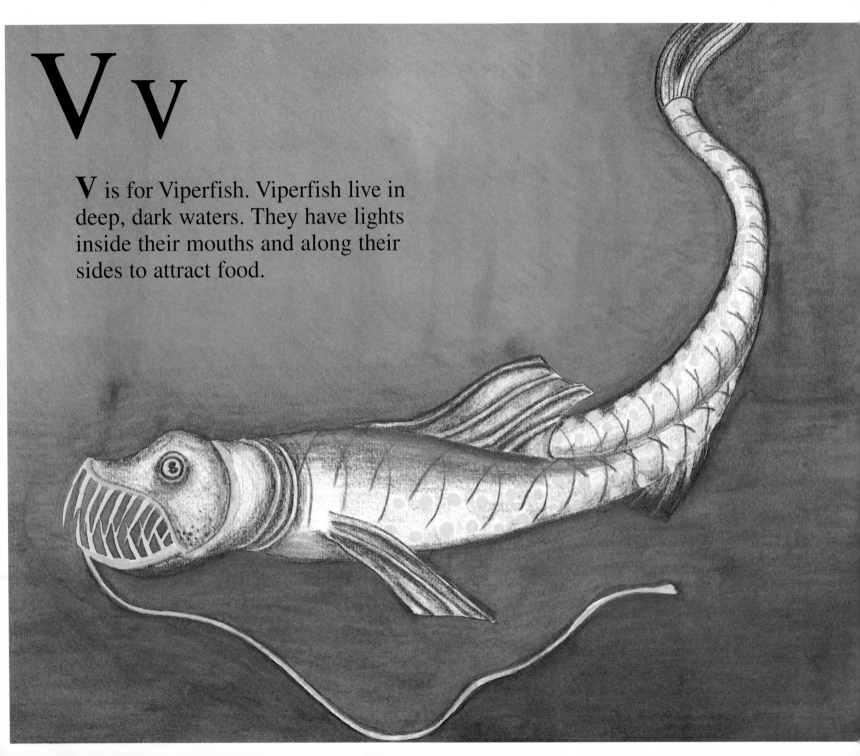

W is for Wolffish. Wolffish have large teeth and strong jaws that are used to open their favorite foods: quahogs, scallops, clams, and mussels.

W w

Xx

We cannot think of any fish whose names begin with the letter **X**! Can you?

X x

Oops, we found one! X is for Xiphias gladius (pronounced "ziphias").
This is the scientific name for Swordfish.

Y is for Yellow-tail Flounder. Yellow-tails are flat fish with both eyes on one side of their heads. They are called Yellow-tails because their tails are yellow.

Yy

Zz

Z is for Zillions. That's how
many fish there are in the ocean!